Up We Grow!

A Year in the Life of a Small, Local Farm

Written by Deborah Hodge

Photographed by Brian Harris

Kids Can Press

**For Jack and Finn, my cherished grandsons, and Alexandra, my amazing niece.
It's a privilege to watch you grow! — DH**

Acknowledgments

Thank you to FarmFolk/CityFolk and to photographer Brian Harris for contributing his lovely photographs to this book. A portion of Brian's royalties will be used to fund FarmFolk/CityFolk's programs. FarmFolk/CityFolk Society is a nonprofit organization that works with farm and city to cultivate a local, sustainable food system by developing projects that provide access to, and protection of, food lands; support local, small scale growers and producers; and educate, communicate and celebrate with local food communities. Please see www.ffcf.bc.ca.

Thank you also to Tim Carter, Production Coordinator, Centre for Sustainable Food Systems, UBC Farm, University of BC, for his thorough review of the manuscript. In addition, we are grateful to Chris Bodnar, Alyson Chisholm and all the wonderful farmers at Glen Valley Organic Farm Cooperative, Abbotsford, BC, for giving us a close-up view of sustainable farming in action.

Finally, a heartfelt thank you to our editor, Sheila Barry, for her enthusiastic support of this book.

Text © 2010 Deborah Hodge
Photographs © 2010 Brian Harris

Kids Can Press acknowledges the financial support of the Government of Ontario, through the Ontario Media Development Corporation's Ontario Book Initiative; the Ontario Arts Council; the Canada Council for the Arts; and the Government of Canada, through the BPIDP, for our publishing activity.

Published in Canada by
Kids Can Press Ltd.
29 Birch Avenue
Toronto, ON M4V 1E2

Published in the U.S. by
Kids Can Press Ltd.
2250 Military Road
Tonawanda, NY 14150

www.kidscanpress.com

Edited by Sheila Barry
Designed by Julia Naimska

This book is smyth sewn casebound.
Manufactured in Singapore, in 3/2010 by Tien Wah Press (Pte) Ltd.

CM 10 0 9 8 7 6 5 4 3 2 1

Library and Archives Canada Cataloguing in Publication

Hodge, Deborah
    Up we grow! : a year in the life of a small, local farm / written by Deborah Hodge ; photographs by Brian Harris.

ISBN 978-1-55453-561-3

1. Farms, Small — Juvenile literature. 2. Farm life — Juvenile literature. 3. Sustainable agriculture — Juvenile literature.
4. Organic farming — Juvenile literature. I. Harris, Brian, 1951– II. Title.

S519.H56 2010   j630   C2009-906785-4

Kids Can Press is a *Corus*™ Entertainment company

FSC
Mixed Sources
Product group from well-managed
forests, controlled sources and
recycled wood or fibre
Cert no. DNV-COC-000025
www.fsc.org
© 1996 Forest Stewardship Council

SPRING

SUMMER

On a small farm not too far from the city, farmers are growing healthy, delicious food for you and me to eat. All through the year — spring, summer, fall and winter — the farmers lovingly care for the plants and animals that give us our food.

Would you like to visit the farm? Pull on your boots, grab a hoe and let's go!

FALL

WINTER

SPRING

It's spring on the farm, and the signs of new life are everywhere!

As the warm sun heats up the land, tiny creatures stir below the ground. The grass is growing, and green leaves are sprouting on the trees. Robins are chirping. Baby animals are being born. "Maa, maa," the new goat kid calls to its mother.

In the fields, the farmers are plowing the soil and getting ready to plant the seeds that will grow into our food.

What kind of seed would you like to plant?

Caring for the Land
Almost everything we eat begins as a plant that grows in the soil, or as an animal that eats the plants that grow in the soil. Fruits, vegetables, wheat, milk, eggs and meat all come from the land. When farmers take care of the land, they are also taking care of our food.

On this small farm, a group of farmers and their supporters own the land together. The farmers grow food for themselves and to sell to people who live in the cities and towns nearby.

Owning the land together lets the farmers share the work, the worries and the satisfaction of growing fresh, healthy food.

There are many jobs on the farm, so the farmers divide up the work. One farmer raises chickens and collects eggs. Another farmer grows salad greens. Others tend the fruits and vegetables, or milk the goats and make cheese. Everyone takes a turn selling the food at the farmers' market.

Which job would you like best?

Spring is planting time. The farmers sow the seeds and plant the little seedlings that give us our food. They grow many different kinds of fruits and vegetables. Some are planted each spring, while others grow back year after year.

The seeds and seedlings are sown in rich soil, in rows. Warm sun and careful watering help them grow. Hoses with tiny holes are placed along the rows. They keep the soil moist without using too much water.

These children are planting seed potatoes. Some of last year's potatoes were saved so that they could be cut into sections and buried in the soil. Before long, leafy, green plants will spring up, with tender, new potatoes forming below the ground.

How do you like your potatoes? Baked and stuffed with cheese? Mashed with melting butter? Or cut into wedges and roasted? Mmm ... oven fries!

Soil is the living dirt that plants grow in. Healthy soil is made up of many things: crumbling rocks, tiny creatures, water, air, and rotting plant and animal matter.

As plants grow, they use up some of the soil's food. The farmers feed the soil and make it healthy by adding compost: a mixture of wood chips, animal manure, and rotted plant and vegetable matter that they collect all year.

Do you have a compost bin?

The farmers also place mulch around the plants. This covering of sawdust, straw or reusable plastic keeps the soil moist and warm, and it keeps the weeds away. Some mulches feed the soil, too!

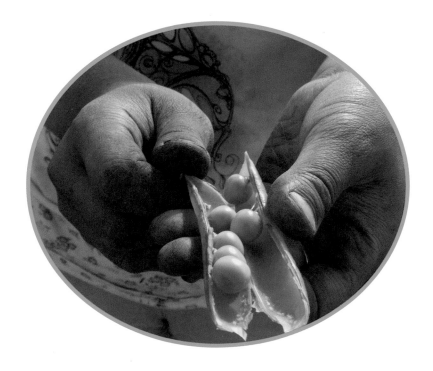

Caring for the Soil
When farmers feed the soil and keep it healthy, they are working with nature to care for the plants and animals that give us our food. If the soil is healthy, so is our food.

SUMMER

It's summer on the farm, and everything is growing!

Hot, sunny days make the plants grow thick and tall. The raspberries are juicy and red. Plump pea pods hang from the vines. Sweet corn is stretching up, and tiny apples are forming in the trees. A rooster crows, pigs grunt, bees buzz and a tractor hums. Frisky goat kids leap and play.

In the fields, the farmers are busy tending the plants and picking the fruits and vegetables that are ripe and ready to eat.

You're growing, too! How big are you?

Caring for Animals

The baby animals, born in the spring, are growing up healthy and happy.

They have good food, safe shelters and lots of space to roam. The farmers take care of the animals and treat them well.

The animals wander outdoors in the warm sunshine. The chickens scratch the ground, looking for tasty bugs to eat. The goats gobble up grass and play chase with one another. The fresh food helps the goats make rich milk. The chickens lay eggs with bright orange yolks.

How do you care for your animals?

The farmers plant bright, beautiful flowers among the vegetables. These flowers attract birds and helpful insects to feed on tiny pests that harm the crops.

Bzz, bzz ... This bee is collecting sweet nectar to turn into honey. As it flies, it spreads pollen (flower dust) among the flowers. The pollen helps the flowers make seeds or grow into fruit with seeds. Bees are the farmers' friends!

The farmers work long days in the hot sun. Up and down the rows they go, digging potatoes, pulling up onions, picking strawberries, cutting lettuce, snapping beans and loading all the tasty food into bins.

Juicy peaches, crunchy carrots or sweet, ripe cherries. What's your favorite summer food?

The farmers wash the fruits and vegetables at the washing station and then load them into boxes to go to the farmers' market.

Other farmers are hard at work in the fields, hoeing weeds, picking pests off the plants and sowing new rows of seeds that will sprout into winter crops.

On a warm summer weekend, the farmers and their families take a break and have a feast to celebrate their hard work and the beautiful bounty of the farm.

The farmers cook the meal in a big country kitchen. The food is fresh and delicious. There are platters of creamy cheese and devilled eggs, bowls of potato salad and spinach salad, hot, buttered corn, roasted vegetables, barbecued chicken and — best of all — raspberry pie baked with berries picked that morning. It's all washed down with frosty pitchers of chilled goat's milk.

Everyone — especially the kids and dogs — has fun! They eat, play games, make music and dance. The party goes on until dark.

How do you like to celebrate?

Caring for Each Other
When farmers work and celebrate together, they can help each other and share in the joy of caring for the land. Older farmers teach the younger ones, and everyone, including the children, takes part in the important work of growing food.

FALL

It's fall on the farm, and it's harvest time!

As the days get shorter, the night air turns chilly. The leaves on the trees are changing color, and the birds fly away to a warmer place. "Honk, honk, honk," call the geese. The goats grow shaggier coats. The chickens lay fewer eggs.

In the fields, the farmers harvest the last of the fruits and vegetables — bright orange pumpkins, yellow squashes, green grapes, red apples and purple plums.

The farm is alive with color!

What colors do you see in fall?

At harvest time, the farm families are busy preserving food. They make juice from apples, pies from pumpkins and jam from fruit. They store potatoes, carrots and other root vegetables in a cool place. They gather honey from the hives. The farmers work hard to give us food for winter.

When it rains, the chickens stay dry inside the hen house. "Bok, bok, bok," they cluck. The farmers carefully collect their eggs, wash them and pack them into egg cartons to sell.

On cold or wet days, the goats cuddle in the goat house and munch on hay. The farmers milk them every day. Some of the milk is for drinking. The rest is made into soft, creamy cheese.

The farmers harvest honey from the beehives and pour it into jars. Each jar of honey tastes like the flowers the bees visited.

Honey is yummy! How do you like to eat it? In a honey ice cream cone? Drizzled on pancakes? Or baked in a sweet honey cake?

The farmers load the food into trucks and drive it to the farmers' market. They sell the food to people who live in cities and towns near the farm.

The market is a bustling, outdoor space, with long rows of tents and tables loaded with fruits and vegetables. The shoppers chat with the farmers and get to know the people who grow their food.

Zucchinis, apples, berries, bread, pies, tomatoes, pumpkins, plums, eggs, meat, honey, cheese — almost every fresh, local food you can imagine is for sale. The food is in season, so it's ripe, delicious and good for you. Fresh food is healthy food. It helps you grow!

Families bring their dogs, kids get their faces painted and musicians play music. Everybody celebrates food!

Is there a farmers' market where you live?

As they harvest, the farmers add vegetable trimmings to the compost pile. The compost becomes rich and dark, and full of goodness.

Some farmers collect seeds from the bean, pea or tomato plants they grew. They will save the seeds to plant next year.

When the harvest is done, the farmers plant cover crops of clover, oats or winter peas. Cover crops feed the soil and hold it in place over winter. They also keep the weeds away. Next spring, the farmers will plow the cover crops into the soil, making it healthy and ready for growing again.

Winter, spring, summer or fall. What's your favorite season of all?

Caring for the Earth
The farmers care for the land all year long. Compost is collected, the soil is nurtured and water is carefully used. When farmers farm in harmony with nature and the seasons, they are helping to care for the earth and all the creatures who share it with us.

WINTER

It's winter on the farm, and the soil is resting.

The days turn short and cold. The branches on the trees are bare, and a blanket of snow covers the fields. The farm is quiet and beautiful. The goats wander outside to nibble on tasty blackberry bushes, but the chickens stay cozy and snug in their hen house.

The farmers repair tractors, buildings and fences. They prune the fruit trees. They make sure all the farm animals have warm shelter, clean water and extra food.

How do you keep warm in winter?

Winter is a time to plan for spring. The farmers decide what to grow and where to plant. They move their crops around each year to keep the soil healthy and the pests away.

Winter is a time for sowing seeds in a cold frame or greenhouse. The seeds sprout quickly in these bright, warm shelters. When spring comes, the tiny seedlings will be planted in the fields.

Best of all, winter is a time for the farmers to relax with family and friends and to enjoy the wonderful food they worked all year to grow.

Soon, the snow will melt and the birds will return. Spring will come — and a new year of growing will begin!

Are you ready?

Caring for the Future
Farmers who grow fresh, natural food while caring for the land are also caring for our future. The soil becomes richer, the farmers earn a living and we all grow up strong and healthy, eating delicious food from farms in our own area. Is there a small farm near you?

About This Book and Sustainable Farms

While this small, local farm is a composite one, it is largely based on the dedicated farmers at Glen Valley Organic Farm Cooperative in Abbotsford, British Columbia (see above). Glen Valley Farm and the other farms featured in this book strive to be sustainable farms: small farms that produce a mix of healthy and often organic foods for people and animals.

A sustainable farm nurtures the soil by using environmentally friendly practices that may include composting, mulching, seed saving, natural fertilizers, drip irrigation, integrated pest management, crop rotation, cover crops and humane animal care. A sustainable farm works hard to sustain the land for future generations and to improve the health of the soil every year.

Finally, a sustainable farm aims to support its farmers and provide them with a living, while fostering strong connections with city dwellers who wish to buy fresh, locally grown food.

Thank you to all the remarkable farmers who generously allowed us to photograph them:

Blackberry Wood (musicians at the farmers' market)

Bhumi Farm Organics
C.E.E.D.S. (Community Enhancement and Economic Development Society)
Glen Valley Organic Farm Cooperative
Golden Ears Community Farm
Klippers Organics Acres
Linnaea Farm
O.U.R. Ecovillage Cooperative
Sapo Bravo Organics
Sointula Greens Farm
Terra Nova Sharing Farm
UBC Farm at the University of British Columbia
Vancouver Farmers Markets
World in a Garden Project